For S[...]

MW00938193

TRIPLE TROUBLE PLUS ONE

by
Diane Wander

There's nothing better than
curling up with a good book.

May every new book you read
take you on a wonderful
adventure!

Diane ♡
♡ Wander

Copyright © 2016 by Diane C. Wander

All rights reserved. This book or any portion thereof may not
be reproduced or used in any manner whatsoever without the
express written permission of the publisher except for the use of
brief quotations in a book review.

Printed in the United States of America

First Printing, 2016

ISBN: 978-0-9970558-1-8 (paperback)
ISBN: 978-0-9970558-0-1 (hardcover)
ISBN: 978-0-9970558-2-5 (ebook)

Dedication

For my *Fearless Foursome* without whom this novel would not exist. Thanks for giving me the greatest ride of my life!

TABLE OF CONTENTS

I.

TV Torture

It was a typical Thursday afternoon in the Hoffman house. Within five minutes of arrival home from school, bedlam had erupted. In the kitchen, empty cups of juice and torn bits and pieces of pretzel and potato chip snack bags littered the counters and floor. A trail of crumbs led from the kitchen to the nearby family room. Backpacks had been dumped with piles of crumbled papers, notebooks, and text-books thrown all over the place. Dirty socks, sneakers, and sweaters covered the stairwell leading from the family room to the upstairs bedrooms, where the Hoffman children had been sent to do their homework.

Brown haired, blue-eyed, eleven-year-old Brayden was lying on his bed in his usual pose staring at the ceiling and playing with the rubber bands that connected the upper and lower brackets and braces in his mouth. Just about to doze off, the pounding of feet racing by his door made him jump from his bed. Brayden fumbled for his glasses, straightened his food-stained uniform shirt and wrinkled khaki pants, and walked to his doorway.

"Hey, Jason, where are you going?" Brayden asked.

Brayden, one of three fraternal triplets, watched his brother Jason—a skinnier, shorter, brown-eyed version of himself slide down the banister. Getting no answer, he left his bedroom and ran down the stairs into the family room, where Jason had turned on their new 75-inch 3D Smart LED TV.

"What are you doing?" Brayden asked. "You know we're not allowed to watch until homework is finished."

About to tattle on his brother, Brayden quickly changed his mind when he realized that an *Austin & Ally* repeat was on the tube. He quickly picked up the remote and turned down the volume.

"We're gonna get in trouble if Mom hears the TV," Brayden warned him.

"Not to worry!" Jason said with a smile. "Mom's in the den on the other end of the house checking her email. That'll keep her busy for a while. Besides, she thinks we're upstairs doing homework. Chill, Brayden, and enjoy whatever time we can get away with. This new TV is amazing!"

"Okay, okay!" Brayden said in agreement, "but we still need to keep the volume low…just in case."

But the lower volume did not discourage the boys' sisters. Soon after Brayden and Jason had flopped down on the well-worn leather couch, Maddie, their nine-year-old younger sister, came running down the stairs. Reaching the bottom, she cartwheeled across the playroom.

"Who said you could watch TV?" she shouted. With her long brown braids swinging from side to side, she paused and then added, "If you're breaking the rules, I am, too!"

Right behind Maddie was Rebecca, the boys' triplet sister. Totally unlike her brothers—except for their metal mouths filled with braces, brackets, and iridescent elastic bands—Rebecca had curly red hair, freckles, and tended to be shy.

"What if we get caught?" she asked timidly.

"Just keep quiet, and no one is getting in trouble," Brayden said, although he was not quite sure he really believed what he was saying.

So the four partners in crime settled in for their un-earned TV time, but Maddie had a different plan as to how she and her sister should spend these precious moments. With Brayden and Jason now lying on the floor in front of the tube, she pulled out her iPhone, adjusted her eyeglasses, and texted Rebecca,

Let's take photos of the boys watching TV and send them to Mom!

Immediately reading her sister's message, Rebecca began to laugh but covered her mouth quickly.

Ganging up with Maddie is a great idea, she thought to herself. *Why didn't I think of that first?*

Rebecca moved closer to Maddie on the couch. With cell phones in hand, the two of them began clicking photos of the boys. The more they clicked, the more difficult it was to stop laughing. Just as they were about to send their mother the pictures, the girls were attacked.

"What are you doing?" the boys yelled, as they grabbed at the girls' cell phones.

Brayden then got his iPhone, and Jason went on the offense.

"Get them, Brayden! Take pictures of them down here in the family room *not* doing their homework. I'm sure Mom would love a few 8X10 copies of these for the family photo album."

As Jason and Brayden burst into non-stop laughter, a loud blast from the intercom echoed through the family room.

"Brayden! Jason! Rebecca! Maddie! Turn off that TV, and come here right now! How many times do I have to tell you that there's no TV, iPads, or cell phones until homework is done… and where are your writing competition permission slips?"

Brayden quickly clicked off the TV. Knowing what would happen if they broke the homework rules, they all chose to ignore their mother's angry order to appear in the den and instead pretended to look busy organizing their papers, notebooks, and textbooks, which should have been upstairs in their bedrooms.

Suddenly their mother charged into the family room. With the stern look of a sergeant ready to reprimand her troops, she began to wave a computer printout back and forth.

"Didn't you hear me calling you to come into the den? How many times do I need to tell you that homework gets done first? And what is this e-mail I just received from school about a Spring Language Arts Fair? All of you should have received a permission slip for an 'All About Me' writing competition being sponsored by a major publishing company. This is a very big deal! *All of you are going to participate!*" she said loudly.

The foursome began to groan, but as their mother continued yelling, it was obvious she didn't hear them at all.

"How is it possible that not even one of you showed it to me? The permission slip is due tomorrow! Do any of you even have it? *Check your book bags now!*" she shouted.

The kids scrambled to the floor and began tearing apart their book bags. While Rebecca and Maddie slowly examined each folder, the boys' crumbled papers flew in all directions.

"What a mess!" Mrs, Hoffman said. "Aren't you embarrassed, boys? You're in sixth grade! Can't you keep your book bags organized? Open up each of those crumbled papers and find your permission slips, now!"

As Brayden and Jason sorted through their pile, their mother stood with her arms folded tapping her foot impatiently. When all hope seemed to be lost, Rebecca, the most organized of the foursome, found her permission slip.

"Here it is, Mom," she proudly announced.

Unable to find his, Brayden sneered at Rebecca and said, "You think you're so good, don't you. What difference will the permission slip make to you when you don't even know how to write!"

"That will be quite enough, Brayden," Mrs. Hoffman said, scolding him. "Forget about the other permission slips. I'll just make copies from this one, but none of you are blameless. Boys, I expect these book bags cleaned right now! And after dinner, there's no TV or iPads tonight for any of you because you broke the rules. Better that you spend the time in your rooms thinking about what you're going to write about yourself for the writing contest."

"*That's not fair!*" they all yelled in unison.

"Fair?" she responded sarcastically. "The only fair I care about right now is the one mentioned right here."

Waving Rebecca's paper more forcefully, their mother began to shout orders.

"Everyone into the den to get their permission slip copied and signed! Upstairs to finish your homework! Clean out those book bags! Let's go *now!*" she yelled.

Future Authors of America "All About Me"
<u>Writing Competition</u>

I give permission for my son/daughter
_____ to participate in the *Future Authors of America All About Me* Writing Competition sponsored by Orange Grove Publishing Company. I understand that my child will be required to write an autobiography <u>due no later than December 14</u>. Royal Palm Academy's Language Arts panel of judges will then select the three best entries at each grade level 4–6 for submission to the Orange Grove Publishing writing competition. Winning entries will be published in the Orange Grove *Future Authors of America* Literary Magazine. Winners will be invited to a special luncheon in Disney World, where they will be honored for their achievements and will receive free one-day admissions for themselves and their parents to a Disney park of their choice!

_____   _____
         Parent Signature   Date

**This permission slip is due to your child's
Language Arts teacher on Friday, November 6.**

One hour later, with all orders obeyed and dinner quickly eaten, the foursome was back in their rooms. Jason and Brayden could be heard over the intercom angrily complaining about the boring evening ahead.

"I can't believe we are punished again," Jason said, moaning.

"Well, it's your fault," Brayden said. "If you hadn't turned on the TV in the first place, this never would've happened."

With that, Brayden slammed his door shut and flopped back down on the bed.

"This isn't fair," he mumbled to himself. "First, we lose television, then iPads, and now we have to enter some dumb writing contest. I don't care what Mom says. I'm not doing it! I get enough homework. No way I'm volunteering to do more. No way this stupid contest is gonna interfere with football and basketball." Staring at his signed permission slip, he thought, *I don't care that the winners get to go to Disney World. I'm out!*

Brayden threw his glasses on the floor, put the pillow over his head, and fell asleep.

Jason, however, was by no means ready for bed. While playing games on his cell phone and texting his friends to find out whether their parents were making them enter the writing contest, he raided the secret pile of Halloween candy he had hidden under his mattress. There was nothing like *Twix* chocolate bars and *Nerds* to comfort him on an evening without electronics.

On the other side of the hallway, Rebecca was still doing her homework, which gave Maddie the chance she was waiting for. Knowing her older sister was totally focused on her work, Maddie ran into the bathroom shouting, "I've got first dibs on the shower tonight!"

"Not fair!" Rebecca replied angrily. "It's my turn to go first."

"You snooze, you lose." Maddie laughed as she slammed the bathroom door and turned on the shower.

"I hate her so much!" Rebecca said in frustration. "Tomorrow night, the bathroom is mine!"

❧

While the Hoffman foursome moaned and groaned in their upstairs bedrooms, Dr. and Mrs. Hoffman were in the den. As Mrs. Hoffman prepared Language Arts lesson plans for her fifth grade students at their neighborhood elementary school, Dr. Hoffman was skimming the latest dental magazine and listening to their children's conversations on the intercom.

"Deb, are you listening to what they are saying?" Dr. Hoffman asked his wife. "I'm not sure this writing competition is a good idea. Why do they have to enter? It's voluntary. Right?"

Mrs. Hoffman sighed. "Yes, it is voluntary, but I really think writing an autobiography is a wonderful idea, especially for our kids who are always lumped together as *the triplets* or as *the triplets plus one*. Writing about themselves will give them the chance to express themselves as individuals and hopefully celebrate all the different things that make them special. I know our kids will fight us until the end, but I do really think it's worth it."

"If you think so, then it's okay with me," Dr. Hoffman responded. "But just be prepared for some battle wounds along the way!"

2.

TGIF... THANK GOD IT'S FRIDAY!

Friday dawned, and with its arrival, the Hoffman foursome greeted the day with new energy. Since the weekend ahead promised to be a good one, all they had to do was get through this final seven-hour school day. Fridays felt like torture as the minute hand on the clock seemed to move at a snail's pace. On this particular Friday, however, time seemed to move rapidly. An assembly kicking off the autobiography writing competition resulted in the cancellation of morning classes and the weekly Friday test schedule. In Language Arts, the entire time was devoted to all the rules for the writing contest. With no classwork to complete, students pretended to pay attention. While their fingers were clicking away underneath their desks, student heads could be seen bobbing up and down as new text messages hit their cell phone screens.

At 3:30 PM, the final bell rang. Eager for the weekend to begin, the students ran to their lockers. In the parking lot, Mrs. Hoffman moved ahead slowly in the carpool line while playing *Words With Friends* on her cell phone. When the students barged out of the building, Mrs. Hoffman turned her attention to the exit doors, where her foursome was making their way out. Looking at them from afar, she couldn't believe how much they had grown. Jason and Brayden, her triplet sons, would graduate from sixth grade this year. Rebecca, their triplet sister, was one year behind in fifth grade but was doing well despite early difficulties with learning to read and write. And Maddie, her youngest daughter, was now in fourth grade.

Where have all the years gone? she thought to herself.

It seemed like just yesterday when she and her husband, Scott, were pushing the four of them in double strollers

How cute they all looked back then in their pink and blue matching outfits, she recalled with a smile on her face. *They wouldn't be caught dead like that today!*

As she laughed to herself, her thoughts were brought back to the present with her the arrival of her children.

"I call shotgun," Brayden announced. "No, you had the front on the way to school. It's my turn," Jason said.

"Actually, it's Rebecca's turn," Mrs. Hoffman responded. "Brayden, move to the back."

Brayden moved but not before he gave Rebecca a push as she waited for the prized front seat.

As all four settled into the minivan and dumped their book bags wherever space could be found, Jason called from the back of the van, "Mom, what about the car pool line no cell phone rule? Do you think you're special?"

"Who's the mother here, Jason?" Mrs. Hoffman said. "How many times do I need to tell you to be respectful?"

"But, Mom—"

Just as Jason was about to answer back, his mother cut him off.

"And speaking of cell phones, your guidance counselor called me today."

Silence filled the car.

"She told me that you have had three warnings about using your cell phone in school. You know what that means, Jason…no cell phone for you all weekend!"

"That's not fair!" he yelled. "Brayden uses his cell phone all the time in school, but he never gets caught. He should have his cell phone taken away, too."

"It doesn't work that way, Jason. You're the one who got caught, so you pay the price. And besides, you know I hate tattling! If Brayden is using his cell phone and continues to do so, he'll eventually get caught. But I am sure Brayden is listening very carefully and will hopefully learn a lesson from you."

Mrs. Hoffman stared at Brayden through her rear view mirror and added, "Isn't that right, Brayden?"

Brayden did not answer and ducked down in his seat. Out of his mother's eyesight, he delivered a quick jab to Jason's arm.

"Ouch! Brayden just punched me, Mom! He should get punished for that. What about the Hoffman *Use words, not fists* policy?"

"Enough, you two! I can't drive and referee at the same time. You're making me crazy! Maybe it's time for you kids to take the school bus in the afternoon as well as the morning. Keep it up, and there will be no movie tomorrow!"

There was utter silence once again.

No way we're going to miss movies at the mall, Brayden thought to himself.

Just thinking about the popcorn oozing with butter made his mouth water, but his daydreams did not last long. Visions of popcorn were replaced by his mother's stern voice.

"Did you kids remember to bring home instructions for the *All About Me* writing competition?" she asked.

Not expecting a response, she added sarcastically, "Well, just in case you forgot to take them home, the school was smart enough to send another e-mail today with the directions attached. This time, we are all going to be on top of this project, and that means starting this Sunday. Don't plan on going anywhere. When you finish your homework on Sunday, you'll start writing your autobiographies. Just think! You could all become *Future Authors of America*!"

Groans and moans filled the car. As they continued their drive home, all Brayden could think about was that his mother had just ruined his weekend.

Thirty-six hours from now, he thought to himself, *we're all gonna be sent to our rooms so Mom can fulfill her dream of the Hoffman Fabulous Four becoming authors. What a joke!*

3.

TGIS....Thank God It's Saturday!

Saturday morning's arrival couldn't come quick enough for Brayden and Jason. As soon as the sun came peeking through their window shades, they jumped out of bed. Unlike school days when getting up was so painful, Saturdays were the best. Since their mother didn't nag them about homework, they were free to play ball, go to Miami Hurricane football games, hang out at the mall, or just veg in the family room watching TV or playing their favorite video games.

This Saturday was especially welcomed, as they couldn't wait for their afternoon trip out to lunch and the movies at the mall. So...with no time to lose, the boys raced down the stairs ready to battle each other in *Madden 15* before breakfast. With Mom, Dad, and the girls still asleep, they had the entire family room to themselves and intended to take advantage of the peace and quiet.

"No way you're gonna beat me today, Jason. I've got this game all planned out. You are toast!" Brayden bragged.

"Yeah, sure, Brayden," Jason responded sarcastically. "There is no way this thing you have with *strategy* will be any match for my speed and accuracy. Besides, you have no coordination. Do you really think anyone with pathetic eyesight and clumsy hands like yours could beat a skilled player like me?"

"I'm telling on you!" Brayden shouted. "You're not supposed to make fun of my eye and hand problems."

"Why not?" Jason shot back. "You do the same thing to Rebecca all the time. You always make fun of her reading and tell her she's stupid. So why shouldn't you get a dose of your own medicine?" Jason asked.

"Well, Rebecca *is* dumb! She stayed back a year in school, didn't she?" Brayden asked.

"That may be true, but she can't help it if she's stupid," Jason said. "You just shouldn't throw it in her face all the time that she's only in 5th grade."

"Well…aren't you Mr. Nice Guy?" Brayden responded sarcastically. "Since when did you become Rebecca's defender? You're supposed to be on my side, not hers."

"Come on already!" Jason yelled. "Let's just play."

"Well, I'm not playing with you if you won't take back what you said about me," Brayden replied, crossing his arms and stamping his foot.

Hearing the shouting echoing from the family room to the second floor, Rebecca came running down the stairs from her bedroom and called out victoriously, "Ha ha, Brayden. Jason is on my side, not yours! And you *are* clumsy, just like Jason said."

As she plopped down on the couch, a smug smile crossed Rebecca's face. But her victory didn't last long, as Brayden pounced on the couch and punched her in the stomach.

"Ouch!" Rebecca cried.

Holding her stomach and crying, Rebecca ran out of the family room. Through the kitchen, living room, and into the long hallway that led to her parents' bedroom, Rebecca sobbed.

"Mom! Dad! Brayden just punched me. My stomach hurts so-o-o much!"

With a sigh of frustration, Mrs. Hoffman sat up in bed and groaned. "Can't you kids ever act civilized?"

"But Brayden punched me! Don't you care that he hurt me?"

Rebecca ran around to her father's side of the bed and pulled on the blanket covering his head. "Help me, Dad! Mom doesn't care. Brayden shouldn't get away with this."

Unhappy about being awakened early on a Saturday morning, Dr. Hoffman slowly opened his eyes.

Getting angry, Mrs. Hoffman shouted at her husband. "Come on, Scott. Get up! I am not handling this one alone. These kids are like animals. Get out of bed so we can get them back in their cages."

"Why am I an animal? I didn't do anything wrong," Rebecca whined.

"Yes, I am sure you are a perfect angel, just like your brothers," Mrs. Hoffman snapped. "Your father and I will get to the bottom of this right now."

Quickly putting on her bathrobe and slippers, Mrs. Hoffman stomped through the house into the family room, with Dr. Hoffman trailing behind barefooted in a pair of wrinkled, striped shorty pajamas. Seeking protection from her enemies, Rebecca grabbed her father's hand as they entered the family room.

"Okay, boys, what's going on this time?" Dr. Hoffman barked.

"Brayden, did you punch Rebecca in the stomach?" Mrs. Hoffman asked sternly.

"It's not my fault," Brayden whined. "Jason started it. He called me clumsy and pathetic."

"Did not!" Jason shouted. "I said his eyesight was pathetic and his hands were clumsy. That's not the same."

"What's all this got to do with punching Rebecca in the stomach, Brayden?" Dr. Hoffman asked.

"Rebecca called me clumsy, too, and laughed at me. So I punched her. Serves her right!" Brayden said. "And just so you know everything, Jason thinks Rebecca is stupid, too."

Rebecca's tears were now in full force. In between sobs, she shouted, "BRAYDEN CALLED ME DUMB! I heard him tell Jason when I was still upstairs…and said that was why I was kept back in school."

In the only bedroom occupied above, Maddie unhappily left her warm, cozy bed. Knowing that the noise coming from the family room would make sleep no longer possible, she quickly found her glasses and made her way to the battleground below.

As she came down the stairs, she yelled at Rebecca, "All you ever do is cry. Maybe if you weren't such a crybaby, people wouldn't think you were dumb."

"ENOUGH ALREADY! I HAVE HAD JUST ABOUT ALL I CAN TAKE FROM ALL OF YOU!" Mrs. Hoffman shouted. "Why can't you get along with one another? What have we done wrong, Scott? How could we have raised four such unfeeling and cruel children?"

"Mom, I don't know why you're mad at me." Jason smiled. "Unlike Brayden, I remembered the Hoffman *Use words, not fists* policy."

"This is not a time for your jokes, Jason," Dr. Hoffman responded sternly.

"How many times have we had the same conversation about the abusive power of words?" Mrs. Hoffman asked in frustration.

"We know, Mom. *Words can hurt*," Brayden said, in a tone that suggested he had heard his mother say this a million times before.

"Well, words do hurt, Brayden! Especially yours!" Rebecca shouted in between sobs and sniffles.

Mrs. Hoffman looked at Rebecca and continued her lecture.

"You're right, Rebecca, but all of you are guilty of saying hurtful things. Standing in front of your father and me are four bullies in the making. What's amazing to me is that you're all the first ones to name the bullies at school and camp but can't see what's happening right in front of your faces! Do you not remember from the many classes you attended on bullying what can happen to victims of bullying?"

"Oh, Mom…you're making a big deal out of nothing," Jason responded. "We don't really mean what we say to each other. We're only teasing."

"No, Jason." Mrs. Hoffman sighed in disappointment. "You don't get it. Do you think Brayden thinks it's no big deal when you or Rebecca call him pathetic or clumsy? Do you think Rebecca thinks it's no big deal when all of you call her stupid or helpless? I don't think so. You may think that your name-calling is innocent, but it's definitely not. It's verbal abuse! When one of your siblings is bullied, they are just as much a victim as the ones you know in school or camp."

Silence. For once, Jason had nothing to say, and his three siblings were lost in their own thoughts.

"I believe all of you have a lot to think about," Mrs. Hoffman said quietly.

She paused for a few seconds, and then, looking at her husband for agreement, she said, "Dad and I will still let you go to lunch and the movies, but until then we want all of you in your own rooms. Don't plan on coming out for anything except to go to the bathroom."

Mom had spoken! Surprisingly, however, the foursome did not object. After an amazingly wordless breakfast, they all returned to their rooms until it was time to leave for the mall. Although their lunch and movie outing was a welcomed change from their morning punishment, their Saturday afternoon trip just wasn't as much fun as they had thought it would be.

4.

AUTOBIOGRAPHY ANGUISH

As expected, Sunday arrived with record speed. By 10:00 AM, the Hoffman kids were in their rooms completing their homework. While they worked, their mother marched into each of their rooms with a "hot off the printer" copy of the *"All About Me"* writing competition guidelines. As she placed the rules by their sides, her attempts to give each of her children a hug and a smile were unwelcomed. But Mrs. Hoffman refused to give up. Like a coach before a big game, she enthusiastically announced, "This assignment will be a cinch! All you have to do is write about you. Nobody knows more about you than you. Won't that be fun? And just maybe you'll win the contest and get a free trip to Disney World. So Write On!"

As her words of support echoed through the hallway, Mrs. Hoffman went downstairs to tend to Sunday morning chores. But her pre-game speech was not cheered by any members of the Hoffman team.

"I hate writing and am not doing this," Brayden shouted, as he threw the competition rules on the floor and then stomped through the hallway to Jason's room. As he opened the door, an *"All About Me"* paper airplane came flying at his head.

19

"Ouch!" Brayden yelled.

About to punch his brother, Brayden suddenly stopped. Realizing that Jason had found the perfect way to deal with their writing assignment, he ran back to his room to find his rules and joined Jason on the upstairs runway. Within minutes, airplanes were flying in all directions.

Across from Jason's room, Maddie became curious about the noise outside her doorway. As she stepped out into the hallway, she was forced to duck quickly in order to avoid the next plane in flight.

"What are you doing?" she asked. "Your dumb plane almost hit me in the eye!"

"Almost doesn't count," Jason said sarcastically.

Maddie gave her brother one of her looks of disgust and slammed her door.

Downstairs, Dr. and Mrs. Hoffman's attempts to enjoy a relaxing Sunday morning were interrupted by upstairs air traffic. With a sigh, Dr. Hoffman put down his favorite weekend newspaper and hiked to the second floor runway. Hearing their father's steps on the stairway, the boys raced into their rooms. As Brayden's door was closest, he barged in only to find Brayden sitting at his desk pretending to read his now crumpled writing competition rules.

Meanwhile, Rebecca ran down the stairs wildly waving her copy of the competition rules.

"Mom, I can't do this!" she yelled. "You have to help me. I'll never be able to write an autobiography."

About to burst into tears, Rebecca barged into the den where she found her mother listening to the intercom sounds coming from the upstairs hallway. She could tell by the look on her face that she wasn't going to get much help. Mom was the strict one.

"Rebecca," her mother responded, "I am happy to explain the directions and get you started, but you really have to write it by yourself. It is about *you*…not me and not Dad."

"But I can't do it myself!" Rebecca said, sobbing.

"Yes, you can. I'll help you brainstorm ideas for each part and get you started on your introduction, but then you're on your own. I know you can do it!" Mrs. Hoffman said cheerfully.

While Mrs. Hoffman worked with Rebecca, Dr. Hoffman closed down the upstairs runway to incoming and outgoing air traffic, reprimanded the boys, and checked in on Maddie. Satisfied that the three of them were all on track, he returned to the den. En route, he passed Rebecca on her way back to her room crying about having to write her story.

"I don't know why I need to do this, Dad. Mom knows I have *Dyslexia*. Writing is so hard for me, and my words get so jumbled up! Why can't she help me more? It's not fair. I hate her!"

With tears flowing, Rebecca ran into her room and slammed the door. Although somewhat shocked by Rebecca's outburst, Dr. Hoffman decided it would be best to let her settle down on her own. He went back to the den with hopes of returning to his Sunday morning routine.

Feeling sorry for herself, Rebecca flung herself on her bed and sobbed and sobbed. With no one coming to her rescue, her tears gradually ended. Rebecca dragged herself off her bed and returned to her desk, where she unhappily began to write.

Across the hall, Brayden was also at his desk with pen in hand. However, writing his autobiography was nowhere in his thoughts. Staring out the window at the basketball court below, all he could think about were the things he would prefer to be doing on this school-free Sunday. As his mind wandered back and forth from basketball to video games and the new 3D-LED TV, his body moved from his swivel desk chair to his bed. Although he hoped for a long nap, his wish was not meant to be. Unwelcome sounds from the intercom startled him as he was about to doze off.

"Brayden, can you hear me?" his mother asked.

Brayden's eyes popped open, and he sat upright.

"Yeah, Mom. I hear you," Brayden said, trying to hide a yawn.

"I hope you're not taking a nap. You know you need to complete at least the first page of your autobiography this morning if you expect any free time this afternoon. Get to work, Brayden!" Mrs. Hoffman ordered.

"I'm working! I'm at my desk right now," Brayden insisted.

As the intercom clicked off, Brayden rolled off his bed and shuffled slowly back to his desk to carry out orders.

How does she always know what I'm doing? Brayden thought. *I can never get a break!*

With a huge sigh, he sat down, picked up his pen, and began to write his autobiography.

In the meantime, Jason was writing away. What he was writing, however, was not just his autobiography. That was low on his list of things to do. Instead, he was busy texting his friends with Brayden's cell, since his mother had taken his iPhone. Yet, surprisingly, in between responses, he actually managed to write the required first page of his autobiography. Satisfied with his ability to multi-task and not get caught texting, Jason ran down the stairs with his completed page in hand.

"Mom! Dad! I'm done. I'm going outside to play basketball."

As for Maddie, the youngest of the crew, she took her laptop on her bed and typed her first page. Enjoying the peace and quiet of her bedroom, she was in no rush to go downstairs when she was done. Instead, she put on her headphones, laid back on her bed, and listened to the latest songs she had downloaded.

Weeks passed. With constant reminders from Mrs. Hoffman and sometimes Dr. Hoffman, the foursome worked on their autobiographies. For Rebecca, the process was painful. Despite her many pleas for help from her parents, she knew that that they were not going to give in. So Rebecca turned to her very best friend, Jana, for sympathy and support. During study halls and weekend dates, Rebecca and Jana made time to work together. Just like they were taught in Language Arts class, they peer edited each other's stories, making the writing process easier for them both.

After weeks of hard work, Rebecca's story was done... well, maybe not *finally* done. Her mother always made sure to go over all her work for spelling and grammar mistakes. She and her siblings were not allowed to turn in anything without Mrs. Hoffman's seal of approval. But even with this extra help, Rebecca was proud to say that her story was truly her own.

As for Brayden and Jason, they also took a long time to complete their stories, since basketball or football with the neighborhood kids always came first. Yet, thanks to all of the punishments that kept them confined to their rooms, they, too, met the contest deadline.

And last was Maddie. Little was heard from her when she was writing her story. Even though she was always busy with gymnastics at the Harrison Street Gym where she lived for the mats, parallel bars, and balance beam, Maddie worked on her autobiography for days, never asking anyone for help. The only one who knew anything about what she wrote was her best friend Leslie. The two girls were always together and shared everything with each other, but not with their families. Although her mother had read the triplets' stories in progress, Maddie had refused to share hers. So it wasn't until the contest due date that she finally let her mother read her completed autobiography and check it for spelling and grammar mistakes.

As she finished Maddie's last page, Mrs. Hoffman wondered, *Will any of our children win?*

This question was one that she did not consider for long. She was just so happy that their entries would be turned in on time and that she no longer had to nag or threaten them to get their autobiographies done. The fate of her children's work was now in the hands of the judges.

What Do You Think?

Will any of the Hoffmans have their autobiographies selected by the judges at Royal Palm Academy for the Orange Grove Publishing *Future Authors of America All About Me* contest?

In order to make your predictions, turn the page, read their autobiographies, and then make your decision.

READ ON...........

5.

BRAYDEN'S STORY

*L*et me introduce myself. I'm Brayden Hoffman, but that was *not my name when my life began 11 years ago. At Jackson Memorial Hospital where I was born, I was known as Baby A. "Why Baby A," you ask? Well, that was the name given to me by the doctors, who kept poking me all the time after my birth.*

I was not the only baby born to my parents on that very hot and humid August day. After I was born, my Mom gave birth to 2 more babies—a girl (Baby B) and another boy (Baby C). This makes me a triplet…a fraternal triplet. That means we aren't identical. We are just three babies who happened to share Mom's stomach at the same time.

Life as a triplet has not always been easy. It all started in my mom's stomach where I was forced to share a very small space with my brother and sister. We also had to share a very small amount of food because my mother ate like a bird. She says that eating too much made the three of us go wild. Can you imagine our six fists and six legs punching and kicking her at the same time? Since I was at the bottom of Mom's stomach, I didn't get enough food. Maybe this is why food is so important to me today. I definitely can pack away a good meal. Mom tries to put me on a diet but it never

*works. How can a growing boy survive with-
out pizza, hamburgers, hotdogs with gobs and
gobs of ketchup, triple scoop ice cream cones,
and bagfuls of M&M's? My mouth is watering
just thinking about all of them!*

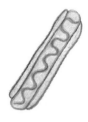

*But let's get back to my first year of life...
After birth, things did not improve much. Besides never having enough to eat, I was forced to wear an eye patch to cure
an eye problem called "Strabismus". This big word means that
my beautiful, blue eyeballs wouldn't stay in the center of my
eyes. They seemed to move inward towards my nose without
my consent. From what I've been told, I was never happy with
the eye patch and spent most of each day pulling it off. When
the eye patch didn't work, they tried glasses which I figured
out how to pull off too. When glasses didn't work, I wound up
having surgery on my eyes not once, but twice! It's a good thing
I don't remember any of this because neither of the surgeries
worked. The first made my eyeballs move too far out, and the
second too far in.*

*Mom and Dad did not take this well.
They couldn't believe my "big, beautiful baby blues" were not perfect. So my
parents took me to Washington, DC to
see America's number one kids' eye doc-
tor—Dr. Pratt. Boy, was his examination
an eye opener (Ha! Ha!). He said that I didn't need any more
surgery, but I did need to be back in glasses which I still wear
today. Although my eyeballs tend to drift at times, nobody
notices. And the best part of the story is that Mom and Dad
took me to Washington, DC every year for the first six years
of my life. After seeing Dr. Pratt, I got to go to the zoo and see
the pandas—Ling Ling and Hsing Hsing. Jason and Rebecca*

were so jealous and still get annoyed whenever I bring up my trips to DC.

Back to my early years when I think Mom was sure I was a genius. How many kids can read at age 3? Well, I did! My preschool teachers were amazed at how well I could read and how quickly I could add and subtract numbers. They always bragged to my parents about how smart and sweet I was. From what I've been told, I was very caring to my sister Rebecca and even held her hand! Knowing my sister today, I can't believe I did anything so dumb. Yuck!

Once I reached first grade, I was put in a gifted program, but no one called me a genius anymore. Don't get me wrong. I still did okay in school, but so many things seemed to get in the way of being an A+ superstar. First, I had the worst handwriting! When I had to write in cursive in third grade, it was really hard. I remember getting so angry when I did poorly on a spelling test. I knew how to spell the words, but my badly formed letters made the words look wrong. I used to get a "C" or "D" in spelling on my report card but win all the school spelling bees. This made me so mad!

Having to answer written questions or write stories frustrated me the most. I would have great ideas running around in my head. But by the time I would get my pencil to move on the paper, Poof! The ideas were gone. Sometimes my pencil cooperated, and I would get words onto paper. More often, nobody could read my writing. Thanks to my very angry right hand, my papers were full of ink smudges, holes, and very messy handwriting. Thank God our sixth grade teachers let us use a computer or iPad!

Mom and Dad have always felt badly that I have had problems with handwriting, but they don't understand why it takes me so long to get anything done. Whether it is doing *my homework, getting dressed, or cleaning my room, I always seem to get sidetracked. Mom says I live in "La La Land." The psychologist says I have "ADD." No…this does not mean I can add. It means I have a problem called "Attention Deficit Disorder." I could take a pill every day to help me concentrate, but Mom and Dad are afraid these pills will keep me up at night. They say they don't have the strength to deal with me during the day and night too.*

So throughout elementary school, my thoughts have wandered. Although it may seem terrible to have "ADD," it really is not so bad. My teachers don't seem to mind if I turn in my work late. My parents are also forgiving. They call me their "absentminded professor." This means that it is okay if I spend extra time staring at a bug crawling on my ceiling or taking a quick nap before finishing my homework. But it doesn't stop Mom from nagging me to get my work done. Sometimes she actually stands right beside me even while I've been writing this autobiography. I know she won't let me quit until she thinks it's perfect!

What I find weird is that I never have a problem concentrating when it comes to playing sports or video games. I am totally "with it" when Jason and I play football. In our  *neighborhood or at summer camp, the two of us have always been rivals. He may be faster than me, but my logical thinking and better understanding of any of the sports we play have made me a winner more than him.*

Win or lose, Jason and I are best friends. We may fight a lot, but we "get each other." We always know what each other is thinking. People say this is a "twin" thing, but if it is, it never happens with Rebecca. Maybe it's because she's a girl…

or it could be because she is always in her room doing her schoolwork. I guess we could teach her a few shortcuts, but those are secrets Jason and I don't want to share.

As for Maddie, she is the youngest and not part of our trio, but I feel closer to her than Rebecca. Although she can be really tough and stubborn, we get along. This is probably because we both have "Strabismus" and have spent lots of time together going back and forth to Washington, DC to see Dr. Pratt and the pandas. Whatever the case, Maddie is okay. Now that she is in fourth grade and part of the upper elementary school, I am not as embarrassed to hang around with her.

Speaking of elementary school, it really has been a blast! This year I graduate from sixth grade, and I really hate to see it end. Mom and Dad keep reminding us that everything starts to count when we go to middle school next year. I'm not sure what that really means. From the looks on my parents' and teachers' faces, I think it means that I'm going to have to pay more attention to my school work. Mom keeps saying it is time "to turn over a new leaf." I have never understood what this means so I googled it last week when I was supposed to be finishing my homework. I found out that the leaves she was talking about are not leaves of a tree. They are leaves of a book. It seems that long ago in the 16th century, people called pages in a book "leaves." When they turned over a new leaf, it meant they were turning to a blank page to start a new lesson. So when people say this today, they mean that it is time to turn over a page of your life and make some changes.

But making change is really hard. When I promise myself I am going to finish my homework on time…or keep my room clean…or stay on a diet, I never seem to keep those promises. So I am not so sure how good I am going to be at turning over a new leaf. However, if I look on the bright side of things, I can admit that I now have a much better idea of what my problems are and know I need to fix them. How are they going to be fixed? I don't have a clue. But Mom always says that "being aware" of what you are doing wrong is the first big step. So I can say proudly that when I graduate sixth grade this year, everybody will be clapping for a very aware Brayden Hoffman. Hopefully, the rest of the steps will follow from there.

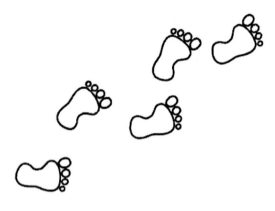

6.

REBECCA'S STORY

*L*ife has always been hard for me. It all started at birth at Jackson Memorial Hospital where I weighed in at 3 lbs. 3 oz. Born five weeks early, I was called "a preemie." The doctors had to hook me up to all kinds of wires so I could breathe. My triplet brothers, Brayden and Jason, got to go home with Mom and Dad after a couple weeks, but I was stuck in the hospital for six weeks! It was a rocky beginning with my weight going down instead of up. Mom and the nurses dressed me in doll clothing because "preemie" clothing was way too big. Even though I can't remember those days, I do have a souvenir—a weird shaped belly button where tubes were attached to give me food and medicine.

My whole first year was a tough one. I had to go back to the hospital twice because I had pneumonia. I was also hard to feed. At each two-hour feeding, I could only drink milk from an eyedropper. One feeding would roll into the next one because I drank so slowly. It was a good thing that Grandma Leah and Grandma Maddie were always around to help out. Mom and Dad said that taking care of my brothers and me was like taking care of wild animals in a zoo! We were all over the place.

Brayden, Jason, and I entered preschool when we were three years old. Where school was easy for my brothers, I had a hard time. At the end of first grade, Mom and Dad decided to send me to another school. There I got special help with reading and math because I was "dyslexic." This means I see things backwards and leave out letters and words when I read and write. I still do this today even though I've been tutored for so many years. I really hate when my brothers and younger sister tease me. They say, "Can't you read?" or "Even little kids can spell that word!" It's so embarrassing!

Anyway, back to my new school. I was much happier there. Learning was so much easier! By the end of third grade, I was ready to move out of the special program for dyslexic kids. So Mom and Dad put me in another school. In this new school they made me repeat third grade. It wasn't a big deal because I liked my teachers, and I got really good grades.

Everything was fine until this year in fifth grade. I changed to the same school where Brayden and Jason go. They are one year ahead of me and tell all the kids that I am different. When I think about it, all the other kids have to do is look at my curly red hair which is always out of place, and they would know I am nothing like my brothers. Mom and Dad and all my relatives tell me how lucky I am to have such beautiful red hair, but all I see is a curly mop that reminds me of spaghetti with too much tomato sauce!

Brayden and Jason tell their friends that I have "special issues" and am not normal. Mom and Dad yell at them and punish them, but they still tell me I am stupid and that they are gifted. When Mom and Dad can't hear, they say so many mean things. Even Maddie, who is younger than me, gangs up with them. It should be the other way around! I am so happy that Brayden and Jason are graduating from sixth grade this year. Next year will be so much better without them.

And speaking of being without them, sleep-away camp is the best! For eight weeks every summer, I get to be with my friends. I don't have to worry about my brothers bothering me. Although Mom makes me get tutored during rest period twice a week, camp is so much fun. I really love to go water skiing even if the water is freezing in the lake. What's really amazing is that Maddie and I get along in camp. At home, we fight over who gets first dibs on the shower or shotgun in the car. In camp, there is no pinching, scratching or pulling hair. It's a real vacation unlike our ski trips or trips to Disney World. There, Maddie and I always have to share a bed and end up kicking each other all night long.

I also love going to art class. Almost every Saturday morning, I go to Mrs. O's art studio to paint and sculpt. For two hours, I don't think about anything but watercolors, oil paint, and clay. You should see the walls of my room. They are filled with my paintings. My brothers and  sister think they stink, but Mrs. O says I have talent. Maybe I'll become an artist when I grow up. I certainly don't want to be a writer!

Grandma Leah thinks I'm talented too. She's the best. When I sleep over at Grandma and Papa's house, she makes me freshly squeezed orange juice in the morning and strains the yucky pulp. Then we go shopping at the mall for the coolest clothing and have lunch at this really great café. Their warm popovers with melted strawberry butter are so yummy!

Grandma Leah is always there for me. When Mom is being mean, I call Grandma. She always makes me feel better. Dad is there for me too, like when Mom makes me do my *homework or this autobiography by myself. Dad tries to comfort me, but Mom is tough. She gives me help but then makes me go upstairs and finish my work on my own. It makes me so angry. Mom always tells me how excited and thankful she was that one of us triplets was a girl. You'd think she would be nicer to me. Why can't she just tell me what to write? I know this is a writing contest so the work has to be my own, but school is hard for me! I get so frustrated. Well...at least Mom is helping me with my spelling and grammar. I would be so embarrassed if I handed in a story with lots of mistakes!*

Now that I am finished, I have to admit that I am happy that I have written this autobiography by myself. I am even happier that I completed mine before my brothers finished theirs. But the thing that makes me happiest is that now that I am done, I am going with Dad to Jaxson's ice cream parlor for a hot fudge sundae with everything on top! TTYL.....

7.

JASON'S STORY

*M*y name is Jason Hoffman, a name that is very well known to family, friends, and fans everywhere. I am most famous for my talent on the basketball court. For the past 3 years running, I have ranked #1 in points per game in our Community Youth Basketball League. This is
really amazing for a player whose nickname is "Little Man." Everyone knows who I am!

But basketball isn't the only reason I am famous. It all started 11 years ago on August 2—a date no one will ever forget. In the early hours of that day, I came into this world, along with a brother and sister. Yes, I am a triplet, and this has always been a big deal to everyone who knows us and to everyone we meet. And out of the three of us, I stand out the most. Although I was last to be born, I am always in the front and center of everything. So...the doctors called me Baby C because of my location in my mom's stomach, but I know that the "C" really stands for "Cool." Mom and Dad would probably add "Cute."

From an early age, I was advanced. I started walking at 9 months of age! Whenever I remind my brother Brayden about *my amazing feat (ha, ha…no pun intended), he shouts back, "At least I'm not a midget or a toothless, old man!" Well, it is true that it took a long time for my teeth to come in. I am also kinda short, but these things haven't stopped me from talking all the time or being a super athlete.*

Mom says I have the "gift of gab." This means I know how to talk to people. She says I could sell ice to the Eskimos! What's amazing is that no one ever made fun of me at home or in camp when I peed in my bed as a young kid. Even my friends at school knew I peed in my bed and never laughed at me. I guess I have always been so funny and cool that I was able to get away without being bullied for wetting the bed. I really was so embarrassed. I feel sorry for kids who have this problem. It is so frustrating not being able to control when you need to pee.

Speaking of control, I also have trouble with my behavior. I may have the "gift of gab," but I talk too much and get grounded. My parents and teachers don't think my non-stop mouth or my behavior is funny. They all think I am in"C"orrigible. This is another "C" word that means my behavior is bad. That is why I spent lots of hours when I was young in "time out" both at home and at school. And now my parents spend lots of time going back and forth to school to meet with my teachers about all the things they think I do wrong. And I wind up stuck in detention. I also have to go to therapy at the psychologist's office. There I discuss my behavior charts that list all the things I've done wrong each week. I am not sure, but I think my parents may be wasting their money taking me to the psychologist. Dr. P. thinks I'm cool. My "gift of gab" seems to be working on him! I think he believes my parents need the therapy, not me!

My behavior may be a problem but not my school work. This is because I am "gifted." School has always been easy for me; well, maybe not that easy. There was that one marking period in fifth grade when I got a "D" in Math. Math was not my best subject so I always left Math homework for last. This really meant I wouldn't do it at all. At the end of the marking period, "Gifted" me got a "D!" Mom and Dad were so angry that they grounded me for weeks. They made sure that every single homework assignment was finished and done correctly. Since that time, I haven't gotten a bad grade in Math. I just can't take the chance of giving them another reason to punish me. I spend so many days grounded in the house without my cellphone, iPad, or TV.

And as I said before, I am great at sports, and not just basketball. I am always one of the first to be picked for a team in school, at camp, or in our neighborhood games. I guess some of the credit for being a super athlete belongs to Papa Sam. He is my hero. Do you know that he set a record for making 76 shots in a row from the foul line? From the time we were little kids, our grandfather worked with Brayden and me every weekend on our athletic skills. Football, basketball, baseball...we did them all. Papa also took us to Dolphins, Heat, and Marlins games. He even brought us to the Super Bowl and World Series! These special events were just for Brayden and me because we were his grandsons—his boys.

While we were at ball games, Rebecca and Maddie went out to lunch and shopping for girl things with Grandma. They really liked that, but I think Brayden and I got the better deal!

Papa has also taught me not to be a quitter. He says that if I try hard, I can be anything I want to be. I'm not sure right now what that will be, but I do know I want to make lots of money. Maybe I'll become a professional basketball player like LeBron James. Or maybe I'll be a comedian. I do keep everyone laughing, especially my sister Rebecca who can never get enough of my jokes! I could also put my selling skills to use and own a big store like Walmart. I don't think I need to decide right now. What I do need to do is end this story so I can go outside and beat the pants off of Brayden on the basketball court!

8.

MADDIE'S STORY

*H*i! I'm Maddie...and no I am not a triplet. Although I get asked almost every day, "Are you one of the triplets?" I am not part of the trio that was born two years before I was born. My story begins nine years ago in September when my very happy mother gave birth to a single baby girl—ME!

Everyone thinks that it must be hard to deal with having two brothers and a sister who are triplets. Actually, it is just the opposite. Mom and Dad spend so much extra time with me so I never feel left out. To make things even better, I am Papa Mike's favorite. I think this is because I was named for his wife—my grandma—who died just before I was born. And just like my grandmother, I am tough. But I have to be tough living with my two older brothers and sister. As happy as I am to have had Mom's stomach all to myself, it hasn't always been easy. Like my brother Brayden, I had to have surgery on my crossed eyes when I was only 10 months old. And just like Brayden, I have had to wear glasses from the time I was a baby. But wearing glasses hasn't really been all that bad. When I was in first grade, I had the coolest pair of red glasses that all my friends and teachers loved. Since I looked so cute in my glasses, they painted a picture of someone who looked just like me in braids and big red glasses in a large mural on

41

the wall at school! Anyway, now that I am in fourth grade, Mom and Dad promised me that I can get contacts when I graduate elementary school in two years. I can't wait!

But let's get back to the hard parts of my life... When I was three months old, I wound up back in the hospital because I passed out—just stopped breathing! Mom and Dad were so flipped out. Well, after two days in the hospital getting all kinds of tests, the doctors couldn't figure out what was wrong with me so they said I had a "fainting spell." When I kept fainting, Mom and Dad decided that these spells were something I had gotten from my Grandma Maddie and my Aunt Suzie. Just like them when they were young, I was able to hold my breath and pass out whenever things didn't go my way. Mom and Dad were so happy when I couldn't faint anymore at age four.

Mom and Dad aren't happy with my stubbornness. Dad says I got this from Mom, but she says it comes from Dad. Whatever! Being tough and stubborn has helped me lots when dealing with my brothers and sister. Even though I am younger, I have always stood up for myself and never go running to Mom and Dad crying like my sister does. But my toughness didn't work out so well for me when I kicked Brayden in his shin last

 *year for being an idiot. I wound up breaking my toe and couldn't go to my gymnastics class for two weeks. This made me so mad! I love gymnastics and am really strong because of all the training I do for team competitions. There's no place I'd rather be than Harrison Street Gym, except for playing with my cat Lucky.*

Lucky has been a part of our family since my 6th birthday so I kinda think of him as mine. That's okay with everyone

else because Lucky isn't the nicest cat and is really big.. He weighs 26 pounds and looks more like a mini tiger than a cat. When we take him to the vet, he not only scares the people and pets in the waiting room but the doctors and nurses, too. Lucky does not scare me at all. I know he likes to play mind games  with anyone who is afraid of him. Lucky will jump out of places and stalk you, but not me. He knows I am boss. When he tries to swipe at me, I stop him and he obeys. Lucky may freak out other people but to me, he is a pussycat.

 Besides Lucky, I have always liked dolls. I think I am getting too old to play with them now, but I am still very attached to them. My favorite one is actually named Maddie. She looks just like I did as a little girl with braids and red glasses. Along with my many stuffed animals, Maddie and all my other dolls take up most of my bed. They do make it hard for me to do my homework or write a story like this one. Mom says I need to work at my desk now that I am in fourth grade. I don't want to because it is more cozy sitting on my bed with all my babies. With my door closed, I can ignore my creepy brothers and sister.

Speaking of fourth grade, it is so cool being in upper elementary now. Although I sometimes bump into Brayden, Jason, and Rebecca, I like the fact that I have a lot more teachers and get to go from class to class with my friends. But what is even better is that eight months from now, I will be back at sleep-away camp waterskiing and doing gymnastics all day long. There really is nothing better than that except for the *yummy smell of chocolate chip cookies that Dad is baking in the oven right now! Signing off...Maddie.*

So Now What Do You Think?

Will any of the four autobiographies you have just read be among the entries selected by the judges at Royal Palm Academy for the Orange Grove Publishing *Future Authors of America All About Me* contest?

Place a checkmark next to the name(s) you predict will be selected for the contest. If you don't think any of the Hoffmans will win, check *None of the Above*.

- ☐ Brayden
- ☐ Rebecca
- ☐ Jason
- ☐ Maddie
- ☐ None of the Above

Explain why you made your prediction(s) below:

_____

_____

_____

_____

_____

_____

9.

WINTER BREAK!

The December 7 contest deadline came and went. With autobiographies finished, students at Royal Palm Academy turned their attention to a much more important event—WINTER BREAK! Thoughts of writing contests were far from their minds.

For the Hoffman foursome, vacation meant two full weeks of freedom! Freedom from homework, studying for tests, enforced bedtimes, and Mrs. Hoffman's nightly book bag inspections. Winter break also meant that either the boys or the girls got to go to California to visit Aunt Suzie. This year it was Rebecca and Maddie's turn, so the boys spent their free time planning the daily neighborhood football and basketball games as well as trips to the movies and Jaxson's ice cream parlor. Although envious of the girls' trip to L.A., where Aunt Suzie would take them everywhere, the thought of two weeks at home without them was a gift in itself. To make the situation even better, Dr. and Mrs. Hoffman always felt sorry for the two kids stuck at home, so they let them do almost everything they wanted to do. And when their parents weren't doting on them, there was always Papa Sam, who made sure to take them to every possible football game, including the Orange Bowl, and to the mall to buy whatever they liked.

With the girls off to the airport, Brayden and Jason decided to move in on their father since their mother wouldn't be back from the airport for a while. They found Dr. Hoffman in the den paying bills.

"Dad," Jason asked, "don't you think it would be a good idea if we take advantage of the fact that all the girls in this family are not here and have some time for the guys?"

Dr. Hoffman looked up from his checkbook and, with a smile on his face, responded, "What did you have in mind, Jason?"

Brayden quickly jumped in. "How about pizza and ice cream, but we can't tell Mom. You know how she is about us eating healthy food."

"She won't care," Jason said. "It's our first day of vacation!"

"Well, pizza and ice cream do sound better than paying bills," Dr. Hoffman responded. "I'm sure your mother will understand. Let's go!"

While Dr. Hoffman put away his checkbook and went to find his car keys, the boys ran to the family minivan.

"Shotgun," Jason shouted.

Surprisingly, Brayden did not object. As they settled into their seats with seatbelts fastened, he closed his eyes and whispered to himself, *"The whole backseat is mine!"*

"What's that you said, Brayden?" asked Dr. Hoffman.

"Uh, uh nothing really…but I was thinking about the kind of pizza we should order. Let's get the works—mushrooms, onions, peppers, and pineapple."

"That's disgusting!" Jason said. "I'm not going for pizza if that's what we are ordering."

"You always get your way, Jason. It's not fair. It's my turn today!" Brayden snapped.

"Settle down, boys!" Dr. Hoffman said, interrupting them. "There's an easy solution. One half of the pizza will be Brayden's choice, and one half, Jason's.

"What about you, Dad?" Jason asked.

You should get a choice, too," Brayden added.

"It's okay, boys. It's your vacation. You can order any pizza you want."

The boys quickly turned to each other with a smile. Knowing exactly what each other was thinking, an unspoken message passed back and forth. "This vacation is going to be an awesome 14 days!"

And just as awesome as it was for Brayden and Jason, it was equally a blast for Maddie and Rebecca in L.A. Straight from the airport, Aunt Suzie took them to the Third Street Promenade in Santa Monica. Each with $20 in hand, they got to walk up and down the promenade and buy souvenirs, ice cream, and cookies while Aunt Suzie trailed behind them talking on her cell phone.

"I can't believe Aunt Suzie gave us so much money!" Maddie said.

"And I can't believe she's letting us walk on our own!" Rebecca added, as she stopped to look back at Aunt Suzie. "Mom and Dad would never let us go by ourselves, so we need to be careful. There are probably lots of weirdoes around here."

"Well...do you see any, Rebecca? I certainly don't. You are such a wuss!" Maddie said.

"Why do you always act as if you are the bigger sister, Maddie? I am two years older than you and should be in charge."

"I don't need to listen to you, Rebecca. I can take care of myself. Let's go already. I want to hit *Claire's* and get ice cream."

Maddie raced ahead but then realized she'd better wait for her sister. "Are you coming or not, Rebecca?" she shouted impatiently.

Rebecca responded angrily. "Yeah, Maddie, I'm coming, but if you run ahead, I'm going back to get Aunt Suzie."

"Ooh, I'm really scared," Maddie said, laughing.

Time flew rapidly. Despite many arguments, the afternoon was a success. Leaving Ben and Jerry's, the girls ran to Aunt Suzie with ice cream cones, chocolate chip cookies, and bags from *Claire's*.

"Thanks for everything, Aunt Suzie!" Rebecca shouted, as she and Maddie dipped into their pockets to give their aunt the rest of the money.

"Keep the change, girls!" Aunt Suzie responded with a big smile.

Could this vacation get any better? Maddie thought to herself.

Yes…it did! By the time their two weeks were up, Maddie and Rebecca had gone to Disneyland, Six Flags California, bicycling in Venice Beach, and had enjoyed three more shopping sprees along the Third Street Promenade. They couldn't wait to get home to tell Brayden and Jason how they'd spent winter break. Boy would they be jealous!

On the morning after the girls' return from California, Rebecca and Maddie made their move. Although they were somewhat jetlagged due to the three-hour time difference between California and Florida, they found enough energy to brag to their brothers about all the amazing things they'd done in L.A. Brayden and Jason pretended like they could care less.

"Big deal," said Jason. "We did all the same things last year with Aunt Suzie and more."

"Besides," Brayden said, "while you were away, we got to go to the mall and out to lunch and dinner almost every day!"

And Papa Sam bought us the coolest wireless game headsets!" Jason added.

"You're lying!" Rebecca said. "We don't believe you."

"You're just jealous of all the things we got to do that you have never done in L.A.," Maddie added.

"Enough already!" Mrs. Hoffman said. "Why can't all of you just be appreciative of the wonderful things you got to do over the past two weeks and leave it at that—although it would be nice to hear a 'thank you' once in a while...and speaking of thank you's, I think it would be very nice if each of you girls wrote Aunt Suzie a thank you note."

"Can't we just text her?" Maddie asked.

"It would be so much faster," Rebecca added.

"No...definitely not!" Mrs. Hoffman said forcefully. "Aunt Suzie went out of her way to show you a good time. The least you can do is sit down and write her a good old-fashioned thank you note on the stationery you never seem to use. In fact, why don't you run upstairs and get that done right now before you forget. And while I'm thinking about it," she added, "I want all four of you up there now getting your book bags ready for tomorrow."

Vacation is over! Time to go back to school! Mrs. Hoffman thought to herself.

A chorus of groans came from the Hoffman foursome. As Rebecca and Maddie slowly climbed the stairs, the sounds of Brayden whining could be heard below.

"Why did Mom have to go and ruin our last day of freedom?"

"Come on, Brayden," Jason responded. "Let's get this book bag thing over with. The guys are waiting outside to play football."

"Okay, okay," Brayden mumbled. "I just can't wait for spring break—only 84 days, 10 hours, 15 minutes, and 30 seconds to go.

10.

MONDAY MORNING BLUES

Monday morning came way too quickly. When his alarm clock rang, Brayden's attempts to silence the beeping sounds were useless. The alarm would stop briefly and then let out higher pitched and more frequent beeps. Unwilling to let his alarm clock win, Brayden found the "off" button and went back to sleep, but his snooze did not last long.

"Brayden! Jason!" Dr. Hoffman shouted. "Get downstairs for breakfast. You're going to be late for school!"

With a loud groan, Brayden rolled out of bed and made his way to the bathroom, where he found Jason half-dressed. Although his brother's usual morning routine included globbing his hair with gel so it would stand perfectly on end and covering his newest zits with acne cream *guaranteed to reduce and disguise pimples in minutes!,* Jason had no time for fussing this morning. Knowing he was already late, he ran out of the bathroom.

Brayden, on the other hand, could not be bothered with acne cream, hair gel, or for that matter, a comb or brush. Forgetting to flush the toilet, he stomped out of the bathroom into the hallway where the smell of pancakes filled the air. Eager for the first batch off the griddle, Brayden returned to his room and quickly dressed in his school uniform.

Pancakes on a Monday? he thought to himself. *I guess Dad must feel bad for us now that vacation is over. I'm out of here!*

As Brayden started down the stairs, Jason flew by.

"No way, Brayden. I'm gonna be first, Jason shouted.

"Too late for first, Jason," Rebecca said, laughing as her brother flopped into his chair in the kitchen. "Maddie and I have been eating pancakes for the past fifteen minutes while you and Brayden were still upstairs sleeping."

"Big deal! We're here now," Jason shot back. "I'm hungry, Dad. Gimme a big stack."

"Me, too!" Brayden shouted.

"Don't any of you know how to say please?" Mrs. Hoffman asked, as she walked into the kitchen. "Your father has to get to the office, but he went out of his way on your first day to make you a special breakfast. Can't you show any appreciation?"

"Thank you, Dad," the foursome said, with smirks on their faces.

And just as the boys settled down to enjoy their breakfast, the unwelcome honking sounds of the school bus brought their breakfast to an abrupt end.

"Breakfast is over," Mrs. Hoffman announced. "Back to school. Get your book bags quickly so you don't miss the bus."

"What about my pancakes?" Brayden said, groaning.

"Too late now," Mrs. Hoffman said, shaking her head. "Next time, get up earlier."

Brayden stuffed a pancake in his mouth and a couple more in his pocket.

"Life is just not fair!" he mumbled.

With food coming out of his mouth and crumbs falling from his pocket, Rebecca walked as far as way from Brayden as possible.

"No way I'm sitting next to you on the bus. You're disgusting!"

Brayden was too focused on not being able to finish his father's pancake breakfast to respond to Rebecca. He slowly walked toward the bus with little hope that his day would get any better.

11.

CONTEST COUNTDOWN

And true to his thoughts, Brayden's day did not improve. During third period, his Language Arts teacher, Mrs. Brown, announced that the writing contest results were in. Royal Palm Academy's team of judges had worked throughout the month of December and even during winter break to select the nine students from grades 4–6 whose autobiographies would represent their school in the national writing competition. Results would be announced at the end of week assembly on Friday.

"I can't believe teachers would waste their vacation time reading our dumb stories," Brayden whispered to Jason across the aisle.

"Shh! She is going to hear you," Jason whispered back.

He tore a piece of paper from his notebook, scribbled quickly, and passed a note to Brayden....

They probably have nothing better to do. Besides, I am sure that mine was the best one and made reading all those boring stories worth it. I'll bet you ten bucks that my entry is selected and yours isn't.

As Brayden read the note, his face began to turn red with anger. Unable to keep his temper in check, he scribbled a response, crumbled the note into a tight wad, and hurled it at Jason.

"What are you doing, Brayden? She's gonna catch us!"

Jason quickly picked the note up from the floor and began to read….

No way you'll win! Just because you think you're so cool doesn't mean you know how to write. I'm so much better than you. My entry will be chosen—not yours. The bet is on!

Just as Jason started to flash Brayden a thumbs up, he felt someone behind him and smelled the sour aroma of Mrs. Brown's breath and stale perfume.

"Busted," Jason mumbled.

"What's that in your hands, Jason? Are you getting a head start on your next writing assignment?" Mrs. Brown asked sarcastically. "Let's take a look!"

As Mrs. Brown read the contents of the crumbled up note, Brayden sunk lower in his seat. *Why did Jason have to start passing notes? Now I'm going to be in trouble, too!* he thought to himself.

With her glasses sitting on top of her gray, frizzy hair, Mrs. Brown peered down at Brayden and Jason and said angrily, "I'll see both of you boys in this classroom at the end of the day. Make sure to be on time!"

The bell rang for lunch. As Brayden and Jason left the classroom, they were attacked by all their friends demanding to find out what they had written in the note. While explaining the bet they had just made, their friend Joey interrupted them.

"No way either of you are going to win this competition. No way any Hoffman will win!" he declared.

"Oh yeah, and why not?" Brayden asked.

"Rebecca and Maddie might be losers," Jason added, "but we're not!"

"Yeah, you are!" Jeremy replied angrily. "The judges are not going to pick either of you, and you can bet they're not going to pick your dumb sister because you're triplets."

"What does being triplets have to do with this?" asked Brayden.

"You really are thick!" Joey said, frowning. "If they pick one of you and not the other, the judges will think it'll hurt the feelings of the one not chosen. So you lose. You guys think you can get away with everything because you're triplets, but it doesn't always work that way. And as for Maddie, they won't pick her either. If she got picked, everyone would think it was a sympathy vote for poor little Maddie who sits in the shadows of her triplet sibs. Too bad, boys!"

Jason, who was never at a loss for words, was stunned. Yet, with his reputation in question, he needed a fast comeback. Looking at Brayden, he knew that the two of them had figured out that the Hoffman foursome was probably "toast" when it came to this dumb writing contest. But there was one place that he and his brother could always shine....

"Well, who cares about the stupid writing competition anyway!" Jason said. "We've got ten minutes to eat lunch if we want to have time to play basketball. And if I remember correctly," Jason said, pausing, "Brayden and I are up on the rest of you gifted sports by five games!"

A smile of complete satisfaction crossed Brayden's face. As Jason high-fived him, they ran into the cafeteria.

At the other end of the cafeteria, Rebecca and her best friend Janna were leaving with their fifth grade class.

"I just heard your brothers got in trouble for passing notes in Mrs. Brown's class," Janna told Rebecca.

"How do you know?" Rebecca asked.

"Hoffman news travels fast, especially when it's about Jason. You know, Rebecca. All the girls think he is so cute," Janna said dreamily "…and…..and the guys think he's cool."

"Do you have a crush on my brother, Janna?"

"NO!" Janna insisted. "I'm just telling you what everyone else says."

"Whatever." Rebecca sighed. "Let's just go before we're late."

When the final bell of the day rang, Brayden and Jason met by their lockers so they could go together to Mrs. Brown's classroom.

"What do you think she'll do to us?" Brayden whined.

"Don't be such a wuss, Brayden. This happens to me all the time. All we need to do is appear very sorry, and this time I think we should use the *triplet card.*"

"What do you mean *triplet card?*" Brayden asked.

"Sometimes you are dumber than dumb, Brayden! I'll just tell her how hard it is to be a triplet…how we're forced to compete with each other…and how it sometimes gets us in trouble…like today in class. Believe me, Brayden. She'll feel sorry for us. Just follow my lead. I know what I'm doing."

As they pushed open the door to Mrs. Brown's classroom, Brayden sighed and mumbled under his breath, *Jason, you better be right!*

"Right on time. Good!" Mrs. Brown said with a smile.

Smiling? Brayden thought to himself. *Maybe this won't be as bad as I thought.*

Just as Jason was about to apologize, Mrs. Brown jumped in.

"Wait a minute, Jason. I have something to say to both of you first. I've given a lot of thought to your misbehavior this morning. Where I am certainly not happy that the two of you were passing notes and not paying attention to class, I have decided to give you both another chance. I know it is sometimes difficult for you two triplets to be in the same class and be forced to compete with each other. I'm going to let it go this time...but never again. Do you understand me? Have I made myself clear?"

The boys nodded.

"Thank you, Mrs. Brown!" Brayden said, smiling ear to ear.

As the boys raced down the hallway to get to carpool line, Jason said victoriously, "What did I tell you, Brayden? The *triplet card* worked just like I said it would!"

Brayden quickly fired back. "*Triplet card?* We never would have been in trouble in the first place if you hadn't started passing notes!"

With a satisfied look on his face, he walked past Jason and thought to himself, *No way Jason's getting the last word today.*

12.

AND THE WINNERS ARE. . ...

The week seemed to fly by despite the nervousness all four Hoffmans felt about the upcoming Friday assembly. Jason had convinced himself that his buddies Joey and Jeremy were clueless. *There is no way the judges won't pick my autobiography,* he thought. *I am the best writer in the sixth grade!*

Brayden, on the other hand, wasn't so sure what the outcome would be. Trying to think logically, he sat at his desk night after night writing and rewriting a list of reasons why his story might or might not be selected. By Thursday night, he was so frustrated with his list that he took his smudge-filled paper, rolled it up in a ball, and hurled it into the wastepaper basket.

"Two points!" he shouted. "At least there is one thing I'm good at," Brayden said out loud, as he plopped down on the bed and went to sleep.

Rebecca gave very little thought to the contest, as she knew her story would never be selected.

I don't have a chance, she thought. *No one is giving an award to a kid who can't read or write!*

And with those final words, Rebecca put the competition out of her mind and turned to her latest work of art.

As she finished her landscape oil painting, she felt all the tension drain from her body.

"Wow! This is really good!" she said with a huge smile on her face. *I may stink at writing,* she thought, *but I am a great artist!*

Maddie also spent very little time thinking about the writing contest. Where the hope of winning popped in and out of her mind, she really was too busy with her gymnastics schedule and homework to waste time thinking about the dumb competition. In one of her passing thoughts, she said to herself, *If I had to choose between winning the writing contest or being named "All Around" in the next gymnastics meet, I'd pick gymnastics any day!*

When Friday morning arrived, there was little conversation at the breakfast table. Sensing the tension in the kitchen, Mrs. Hoffman decided it was best not to mention the contest at all. She was relieved when the honking sounds of the school bus got the kids up and running to the door.

On the bus, however, there was no avoiding the topic. Joey and Jeremy started in on Brayden and Jason from the minute they settled into their seats.

"So I wonder who's going to win today?" Jeremy asked sarcastically.

"Well, we know it's not gonna be the Hoffmans!" Joey answered firmly.

"And why not?" Maddie shot back.

Brayden sat silently, but Jason wasn't going to let his pals get the better of him or his siblings.

"You guys are clueless!" Jason said, as he got up from his seat. "We have just as much a chance as you nerds do. And you can bet your life that the judges don't care that we're triplets and that **Poor Maddie** is not."

Boots, the driver who always wore cowboy boots, shouted, "Down in the seat, Hoffman, or you're off the bus for another week!"

Not wanting to get kicked off again, Jason quickly flopped back down in his seat, but not before Maddie slid into the seat next to him and yelled in his face, "**Poor Maddie?** When did I become **Poor Maddie?**"

"I didn't say that," Jason answered. "I'm just repeating what those losers over there told me and Brayden a few days ago. They think the three of us won't win because the judges wouldn't want to pit one triplet against another. And if you'd win, it would be like a sympathy vote cause you're not a triplet."

Directing her anger now at Jeremy and Joey, Maddie sneered and said, "What planet ejected you from orbit? Do you think the judges—OUR TEACHERS—care about our feelings? NOT! And just so you know, I have never been or never will be **Poor Maddie**! You jerks must have suffered major brain damage when you crashed down here!"

The whole bus, including her siblings, burst into laughter and cheered, "*Maddie! Maddie! Maddie!*"

Jeremy and Joey slid lower in their seats.

"Keep quiet back there, or I'll kick all of you off the bus!" Boots shouted.

But the cheers did not stop. Despite the bus driver's warnings, the students could not control themselves. "*Maddie! Maddie! Maddie!*" they continued to chant, all the way to school. When the bus stopped in the school parking lot, Boots was beyond angry.

"That's it! I've had enough!" he yelled. "You Hoffmans are off the bus all next week!"

"That's not fair!" the foursome shouted in unison.

"It's not our fault! Everyone was cheering, not just us," Brayden said, pleading with the driver. "Why are we getting in trouble?"

"I call it as I see it, and you four are off my bus. Period!" Boots stomped off the bus.

While the rest of the kids piled out quietly, the Hoffmans stayed glued to their seats. Recognizing their advantage, Jeremy and Joey went in for the kill. As they walked past the foursome, they began to chant in a whisper so that Boots, now outside the bus, could not hear.

"Maddie! Maddie! Maddie!" They laughed. "See you later, losers!"

Brayden, Jason, Rebecca, and Maddie got off the bus and walked slowly towards school, stunned.

"Suspended from riding the school bus for a week?" Brayden whined. "Mom and Dad are gonna kill us!"

"I'm dead," Jason said, groaning. "This is the third time I've been kicked off the bus this year!"

"I've never gotten in trouble in my whole life!" Rebecca said. "It's your fault, Maddie. You ruined everything!"

"What did I do?" Maddie asked. "Everybody was screaming. The only reason Boots singled us out is because of you, Jason. You're always in trouble."

Brayden looked angrily at his brother.

"Cool it," Jason said calmly. "I'll take care of this. Let me talk to Boots. He's my buddy!"

"What are you gonna do? Bribe him with a new pair of boots? Not!" Brayden said sarcastically.

"Trust me! I've got this handled," Jason said. As he ran toward the bus, he pumped his arm in the air and shouted, "Go, Hoffmans!"

And true to his word, Jason got Boots to change his mind. He caught the bus driver just as he was about to leave the parking lot. As a master of the art of fast talking, Jason persuaded Boots to give them all back their bus riding privileges...but not before promising to bring him a bag of his father's famous homemade chocolate chip cookies first thing Monday morning.

No big deal, Jason thought. *Dad's got enough cookies in the freezer for an army. He'll never know they're missing!*

Jason raced into school and hunted down his siblings to share the good news. His mission complete, he got to homeroom in the nick of time. There, he and his classmates listened to morning announcements until the bell rang for the long-awaited writing contest assembly.

Thirty minutes later, Royal Palm Academy upper elementary students filed into the auditorium. Where it usually took them a number of warnings before they settled down, it was only a matter of seconds on this very special day. The absolute silence should have been calming but only served to increase the tension in the room. As students began to squirm in their seats, Dr. Roberts, Middle School Principal, walked up to the lectern on stage and took the microphone.

"Good morning, students! Welcome to our weekly Friday morning assembly. I can tell by the unusual silence in the room that all of you are eager to hear the results of our "Future Authors of America All About Me" contest sponsored by Orange Grove Publishing. As you all know, participation in this contest was not required. I am proud to report that 100% of our grades 4–6 students submitted entries. Isn't that just wonderful? Teachers…please stand and give a round of applause for our students!"

Brayden whispered to Jason, "The suspense is killing me!"

"Take a chill pill, Brayden. I've got this in the bag," Jason said.

"You wish!" Brayden replied angrily. "I'm—"

"And let's also give a hand for our wonderful team of judges who took so much time to read and evaluate all your autobiographies."

When the applause ended, Dr. Roberts continued. "So, students, I think you have waited long enough! It is now time to announce the three students from each grade, 4 through 6, whose entries have been chosen to represent our school. Let's begin with Grade 4. Will the following students please come to the stage when I announce your names…

Keisha Johnson,

Ethan Reed Jr.,

and Maddie Hoffman."

When each student's name was announced, the audience applauded, but no one was prepared for the cheers that erupted from kids on Maddie's school bus when she came forward. *"Maddie! Maddie! Maddie!"*

"Settle down, students," Dr. Roberts said. "We are thrilled that you are so supportive of your fellow students, but your applause will be enough recognition of their achievements." As the students quieted down, Jason leaned forward to the row in front of him, where Jeremy and Joey were sitting.

"I guess *Poor Maddie* isn't so poor after all! And for your information, we didn't get kicked off the bus. Hoffmans' rule!" Jason bragged.

Rebecca, however, did not have the same confidence. As Dr. Roberts was about to announce the Grade 5 winners, she knew her name would not be called.

I'm such a loser, she thought to herself. *I can't believe Maddie won!*

Rebecca's fate was confirmed seconds later.

"Let's now move on to Grade 5," Dr. Roberts said. "The three winners are...

Emily Freeman,

Wyatt Parker, and

Daniel Chen.

Please give a round of applause for our Grade 5 team of authors!"

While the applause continued, Jason gave no thought to his sister Rebecca. Since he could only think about his soon-to-happen victory walk, his sister's feelings were far from his mind.

"Grade 6 is next up, Brayden. Get your ten bucks ready, bro! Dr. Roberts is about to announce my name," Jason whispered.

"And now for our final group of winners from Grade 6. This was a very difficult choice for our judges because there were so many excellent entries. But rules are rules, and we could only select three. Will the following students proceed to the stage to be recognized...

Noah Rothman,

Priya Ramesh,

and last but not least...

Blake Thatcher."

But Jason did not listen to the final name. Lost in his thoughts of victory, all he could hear was the applause that he assumed was for him. As Jason started to get up to walk to the stage, Brayden yanked him back to his seat.

"Have you lost your mind?" Brayden whispered. "You didn't win!"

Jason stared at him in disbelief.

Jeremy and Joey turned around and smirked. "Way to go! The Hoffman trio goes down in defeat!"

"I didn't hear your names called either," Brayden shot back.

Stunned by this shocking turn of events, Jason had no words to add. He sat there and felt like he was frozen. He knew Dr. Roberts was speaking but heard nothing.

"Let's give another round of applause for our nine winners. We are proud of all of you and wish you the best of luck. We are also proud of all our students who participated in this contest and look forward to our Spring Language Arts Fair, where all your wonderful work will be on display. Congratulations to all!"

Dr. Roberts concluded the assembly, and the students filed out grade by grade. When Maddie and her class passed by, Jason and Brayden were too wrapped up in their own defeat to congratulate their sister. Rebecca did not feel much different. Although she'd never expected to win, it made her so angry that her younger sister had showed her up once again.

Where the rest of the day was miserable for the Hoffman triplets, it was *Fabulous Friday* for Maddie. In addition to all the attention she got from her teachers, her popularity soared amongst her classmates.

What could be better than this? Maddie thought to herself, and then quickly answered her own question...*THE GOLD!*

The gymnastics "All Around" competition was a few short weeks away. Maddie had lots of work to do.

13.

VICTORY CELEBRATION!

Brayden, Rebecca, and Jason dreaded the ride home from school. In fact, they dreaded the whole weekend. With Maddie's victory, they knew that all the attention would be focused on her.

As they walked to the carpool line, Brayden whined to Jason. "I don't know how I'm going to survive Mom and Dad bragging about Maddie."

"I still can't believe they picked Noah, Priya, and Blake over me," Jason complained. "Priah and Blake aren't even Gifted!"

"And what about me?" Rebecca added. "Maddie will make sure to rub her victory in my face. I hate her!"

When they got to the carpool line, Maddie was already there. Wanting to avoid any discussion of the contest, the threesome stood at the back of the line, but Maddie pretended not to notice. After so many gymnastics meets, she knew how it felt to be a loser. She wasn't going to rub it in.

When Mrs. Hoffman pulled up on the carpool line, Maddie hopped into the car.

"Congratulations, Maddie!" Mrs. Hoffman called out, smiling.

"How did you know I won?" Maddie asked, as she jumped into the front seat.

"Dr. Roberts called me after your assembly this morning. Your father and I are so proud of you!" Mrs. Hoffman said.

Just then, the triplets piled into the van. For once, there was no arguing about "shotgun." Jason, Rebecca, and Brayden were happy to be as far away from the front seat as possible. They did not want to hear their mother go on and on about how wonderful Maddie was. Surprisingly, however, she said nothing, and neither did Maddie. The silent ride home was torture, with twenty minutes seeming like two hours. When they finally pulled into the driveway, their father was home early waiting for them. Maddie jumped out first. As she ran into her father's arms for a hug, the triplets tried to rush past.

"Whoa!" Dr. Hoffman said. "Everybody inside. Family meeting!"

"Come on, Dad! It's Friday! Can't we do this later?" Jason said, groaning.

"Could this day get any worse?" Brayden mumbled to himself, as they all threw down their book bags in the family room and flopped down on the couch.

"Take the sad look off your faces," Dr. Hoffman said. "We know this has been an unusual day for all of you, with lots of hopes, fears, tension, disappointment, and for one of you lots of relief and happiness…"

The foursome stared at their father in puzzlement. Noticing the confused looks on all of their faces, Mrs. Hoffman went in for the rescue. She looked directly at the triplets and explained.

"What your father means is that we understand how tough this day has been for the three of you, but feeling disappointment and jealousy is normal. No one likes to lose. But did you really lose? You may have lost a contest, but you have won so much more. All of you have made Dad and me so proud. Just because the judges didn't select all your stories doesn't mean they weren't good. In fact, we think they were great. In our book, all of you are winners! And because you worked so hard, we think you deserve a victory celebration. So this weekend is going to be just that!"

"We're going to Disney World!" Dr. Hoffman shouted.

The triplets were speechless. They couldn't believe how quickly their very bad day had become so good. Within minutes, they were all packed up and ready to go. Jason, first out of the house, ran for the van.

"Shotgun!" he shouted, but then all of a sudden he stopped. A weird idea popped into his head. *Maybe I should let Maddie get first dibs?*

Surprised by this strange thought, Jason turned to Brayden and said, "Don't you think Maddie should get first choice since she won the contest?"

Brayden looked at Jason in disbelief. *What could he be thinking?*

But just as he was about to protest, Brayden suddenly realized his brother was right. Maddie did deserve shotgun.

"Sure, why not!" Brayden said. "The seat's yours, Maddie."

Maddie was amazed.

Mine? she thought to herself. *Are Jason and Brayden insane? I better move fast before they change their minds!*

Maddie ran towards the van. As she was about to jump in, she stopped dead in her tracks, turned towards her brothers, and without thinking blurted out, "It's really Rebecca's turn. She should get first pick."

"Wow! Thanks, Maddie," Rebecca said.

Not believing her good fortune, Rebecca jumped in quickly to her favorite window seat.

Dr. and Mrs. Hoffman sat stunned in disbelief, too. As the two of them gave each other a shocked look, a message seemed to be sent from one to the other.

Are our children actually acting nice to one another? We should enjoy this while it lasts!

With smiles on their faces, their journey to Disney World began.

Three hours later, they pulled up to the Contemporary Hotel. For Jason and Brayden, there was no time to waste. As they unloaded the van, Jason urged his father to hurry.

"Come on, Dad! Let's just dump our luggage and check in later."

"No!" Maddie and Rebecca shouted in unison.

"We want to go to the room first so we can pick our beds," Rebecca insisted.

"Why do you always have to make a big deal about the beds?" Brayden complained. "We gotta get to the park! Just let Maddie pick her bed first since Rebecca got shotgun in the car."

Maddie and Rebecca looked at each other and realized that Brayden was right.

"Deal!" Rebecca said. "Let's go!"

Once again, Dr. and Mrs. Hoffman were shocked by the way their children were solving problems without their usual arguing.

"Okay, everybody. You all go," Mrs. Hoffman said. "I'll check us in and meet you at the park."

"Thanks, Mom!" they all shouted, as Dr. Hoffman gave Mrs. Hoffman a hug goodbye.

Arriving at the park, the boys raced to Tomorrowland.

"Let's get on line for Space Mountain first," Brayden shouted.

"No way!" Rebecca shouted. "I hate that ride."

"You're such a—" Maddie caught herself.

About to call Rebecca a wuss, her mother's voice suddenly echoed in her mind.

Words can hurt. Verbal abuse is bullying.

"I'm not going!" Rebecca said. "Go without me."

"Come on, Rebecca. It will be so much more fun if all of us go," Maddie said, trying to sound encouraging. "I'll sit behind you..."

"And I'll sit in front of you," Jason added. "It's not that scary."

Surprised by the unexpected support from her siblings, Rebecca agreed, and for the first time in her life, she actually enjoyed a scary ride.

"I knew you could do it!" Jason said, cheering as they ran down the exit ramp to meet their parents. "Mom, you're here!" Jason shouted. "Rebecca went on Space Mountain and loved it!"

"Yeah!" Rebecca agreed. "I was so scared, but I screamed my head off. It was so fun. Let's go again!"

Dr. and Mrs. Hoffman were shocked.

"I can't believe Rebecca actually liked Space Mountain!" Mrs. Hoffman said.

"And I can't believe it was Jason and Maddie who persuaded her to do it in the first place. These can't be our kids!" Dr. Hoffman laughed.

Knowing that the wait for the next ride would be a long one, Mrs. Hoffman found a bench in the shade. Just as she was about to nod off, Rebecca pulled her arm.

"Come on, Mom! It's your turn," Rebecca urged. "If I can go on Space Mountain, you can, too!"

Mrs. Hoffman was horrified. *I hate roller coasters!* she thought to herself. *What am I going to do?*

At that moment, Dr. Hoffman came over to her, took her hand, and said, "Don't worry, honey. I'll sit behind you...."

"And I'll sit in front of you," Rebecca added. "All you have to do is scream your head off, and it won't be scary at all!"

Grabbing Rebecca's hand, she forced herself to say, "Okay, let's go!"

"Awesome!" shouted Jason and Brayden. "Hoffmans rock!"

Forty-eight hours later, they were on the road home. After two fun-filled days in Disney World, a sense of contentment could be felt throughout the car. Brayden was especially happy as he thought about roller coasters, fireworks, and all-you-can-eat buffet restaurants. But as he settled in for the three-hour ride, he realized something was different; something was missing. He couldn't quite put his finger on it, and then it hit him.

We haven't said one mean thing to each other since Friday! Kinda weird. He laughed to himself as he started to doze off. *Maybe we should try this more often....*

For Jason, all he could think about was how cool it was that his entire family had gone on Space Mountain. He couldn't wait to tell his friends about their awesome weekend.

As for Rebecca, she felt relief. Understanding it was okay to feel disappointment and even jealousy, her feelings of anger towards Maddie had disappeared.

Maddie really isn't so bad, she thought to herself. *I can't believe she didn't brag about winning the contest and even gave me first dibs on the car seat! Mom always says, Try a little kindness. Maybe she's right!*

Maddie felt so happy. As she remembered the past few days—winning the writing contest and going to Disney World—a thought flashed through her mind.

Rebecca and I didn't have one fight this entire weekend! Amazing!

With a big smile on her face, she put on her headphones, curled up on her seat, and went to sleep.

And as for Dr. and Mrs. Hoffman, they also breathed a huge sigh of relief after spending a fun and relaxing weekend with their kids. Yet, knowing that peace and quiet were always short-lived in the Hoffman family, they decided to enjoy these last few hours because sooner or later, their fearless foursome would find some new way to make *Triple Trouble Plus One!*

Prediction Check-up

Did you predict that Maddie would be the only Hoffman to win the contest?

☐ Yes   ☐ No

What Should Have happened?

Now that you have finished reading
Triple Trouble Plus One...

1. Who do you think should have won the Royal Palm Academy competition and why?

_____
_____
_____

2. Would you have preferred this novel to end in a different way? If so, how?

_____
_____
_____

Share your predictions, answers, comments, or any other questions you may have with the author.

Write to Diane Wander at:
bridgestobetterlearning@gmail.com

THANK YOU NOTES

~ First, I want to thank my four children, Benjamin Wander, Robin Sherman, Joshua Wander, and Mollie Wander who are now all adults. Although this novel is a work of fiction, their memories of what it was like to grow up in a home as "triplets plus one" helped me craft the personalities and voices of the Hoffman foursome.

~ I especially want to thank Robin and Mollie for all their support along the way. They were always there to offer advice as each chapter was written. I love you both for being the best daughters a mother could ever have!

~ I couldn't have written this book without the guidance of two very close friends and colleagues. Thank you, JoAnn Laskin and Sandra Friedman for sharing your educators' expertise. Your advice after reading my first draft was the encouragement I needed to keep writing and revising.

~ I was so fortunate and honored to have Ellen Brazer, published author of three novels, as my mentor. When I completed my first draft, Ellen sat with me many times while I read aloud *Triple Trouble Plus One*. As an accomplished writer, her suggestions helped me write a better story.

~ I also want to thank Anita Meinbach, Clinical Associate Professor in the Department of Teaching and Learning at the University of Miami, for her expert advice on children's literature. She read my story and advised me on how to revise it to meet the interest level of elementary school readers.

~ And speaking of readers, I was so fortunate to have many volunteer student readers to give me advice. I call these children my "focus group." They read my book and then completed a "Book Critic Response Log." Their feedback helped me so much! Thank you to:

- Zack Brown (grade 8), Dylan Field (grade 7), and Collin Field (grade 5) of The Buckley School in Sherman Oaks, California
- Raquel Zajac (grade 4) and Sarah Schulmann (grade 5) of the Lehrman Community School in Miami Beach, Florida
- Aviah Fajerstein (grade 4) and Mrs. Dearman's and Mrs. Kissell's third grade class at Pinecrest School in Fort Lauderdale, Florida

~ I also want to thank my two illustrators. First is Raquel Zajac, a member of my focus group, who drew many of the pictures in the interior of this novel. Although she is only in grade 4, Raquel is truly talented and will hopefully have a career as an illustrator someday. Second is....Leda Almar. Leda is a very talented Argentinian artist who took time out of her very busy work schedule to create the illustration for this novel's front cover. Thank you both for making *Triple Trouble Plus One* such a beautiful book.

❦ So much behind the scenes work goes into editing and publishing of a book. I am truly grateful to Integrative Ink Editing and Publishing Services who did an incredible job with the editing, book design and layout of this novel. I am especially thankful to Stephanee Killen. As my editor, Stephanee gave me expert advice and was always ready to answer every question I asked. Thank you so much!

❦ Finally, I need to thank my husband Stephen, who was with me every step of the way. I can't count the number of times I asked him to listen to me read aloud every chapter written and rewritten and rewritten! Not only is he the best husband, but he is also the greatest Dad. I love you and am so glad you were always by my side with our "triplets plus one"!

About the Illustrators

Raquel Zajac is a nine year old girl who attends fourth grade at the Lehrman Community School in Miami Beach, Florida. As she loves to write and draw, her dream has always been to illustrate a book. Her wish has come true with the publishing of many of the interior illustrations in this novel.

Leda Almar is an Argentinian artist and illustrator. She has lived in Weston, Florida since 2000 where she has a private studio in which she works and teaches drawing, painting, and ceramics. In addition to *Triple Trouble Plus One*, Ms. Almar has illustrated the books of several Argentinian authors.

CPSIA information can be obtained
at www.ICGtesting.com
Printed in the USA
LVOW12s1908150516
488378LV00001B/1/P